First publication in United States of America 1973
All rights reserved
C.I.P. in back of book
ISBN 0–690–95904–4
0–690–95905–2 (LB)
Printed in Great Britain
Reprinted 1974

The Zoo in my Garden

Story and pictures by

CHIYOKO NAKATANI

Thomas Y. Crowell Company
New York

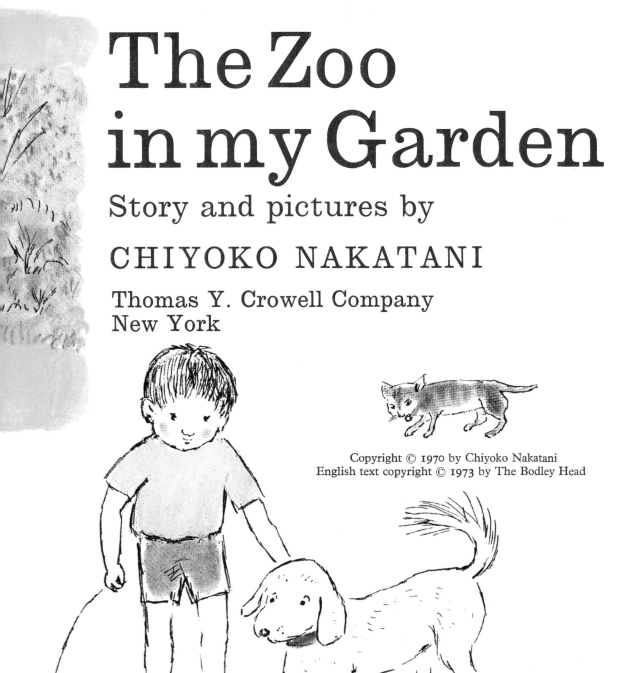

There is a zoo in my garden.
First there is my dog.
He is barking.

His friends often come
to visit him when they
hear him bark.

On the roof of my house
there is a pigeon.
He is cooing to his friends.

His friends come when they hear him coo.
Now there are two pigeons
and three sparrows
in my zoo.

There are tulips in my garden.
Butterflies come into my zoo
to see them.

Often, after the rain,
I find a snail in my garden;
and sometimes frogs, croaking
and hopping.

On the tree at the bottom
of my garden the wasps are
building a nest.
They are buzzing loudly.

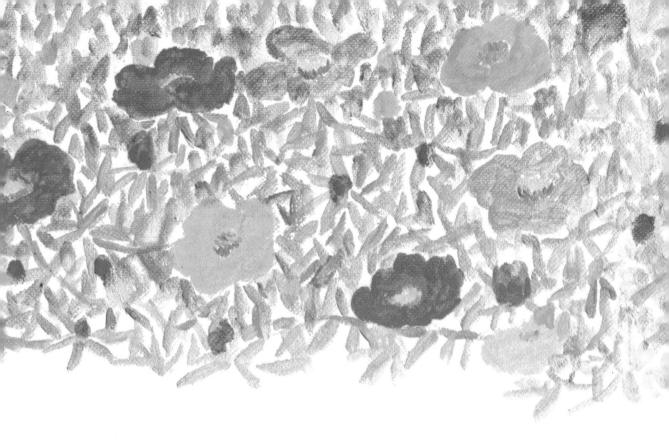

Near the flower bed some ants
have captured a big green beetle.
They are carrying it back
to their nest.

I have another zoo inside my house.
My mother gave me a goldfish
in a bowl.

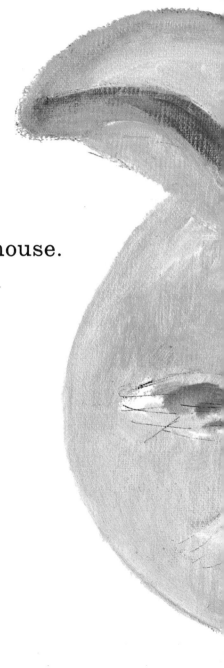

And my father brought me
a turtle.

We also have a parrot,
and we are teaching
him to talk.
"Good morning,
  good morning,
  good morning,"
he squawks.

Walking along the wall are the cats
from next door, a mother and
her kitten. They are meowing,
and the bells on their collars
are tinkling.

The parrot is squawking.
The pigeons are cooing.
And the dog is barking.
What a noise!

Look, Mother,
we have a zoo!

Library of Congress Cataloging in Publication Data

Nakatani, Chiyoko.
  The zoo in my garden.

  SUMMARY: A young boy describes the many animals that
can be found in his garden.
  Translation of Boku no uchi no dóbutsuen.
  [1. Animals—Stories] I. Title.
PZ7.N142Zo3   [E] 72-13921
ISBN 0-690-95904-4
ISBN 0-690-95905-2 (lib. bdg.)